Silvia Vecchini is the author of several picture books and young adult novels, many of which were illustrated by her husband, Antonio Vincenti. In addition to being a writer, she enjoys conducting writing workshops for children and teens. She lives in Italy.

Sualzo (Antonio Vincenti) is a would-be saxophonist and a self-taught illustrator. He has illustrated a number of books by his wife, Silvia Vecchini, including *Breathless* (Tunué), which won the Boscarato Prize and Orbil Balloon Prize in 2012. Sualzo lives in Italy. Visit his website at www.sualzo.com.

For Veronica
and for all the little fish
who are waiting for a phone call

First published in the United States in 2018 by
Eerdmans Books for Young Readers,
an imprint of Wm. B. Eerdmans Publishing Co.
2140 Oak Industrial Dr. NE, Grand Rapids, Michigan 49505
www.eerdmans.com/youngreaders

Text © 2017 Silvia Vecchini
Illustrations © 2017 Sualzo

Originally published in Italy in 2017 under the title *Telefonata con il pesce*
by Topipittori
viale Isonzo 16, 20135 Milan, Italy
www.topipittori.it
English-language edition © 2018 Eerdmans Books for Young Readers

Manufactured in China

27 26 25 24 23 22 21 20 19 18   1 2 3 4 5 6 7 8 9

ISBN 978-0-8028-5510-7

A catalog record of this book is available from the Library of Congress.

PHONE CALL WITH A FISH

Written by
Silvia Vecchini

Illustrated by
Sualzo

Eerdmans Books for Young Readers

Grand Rapids, Michigan

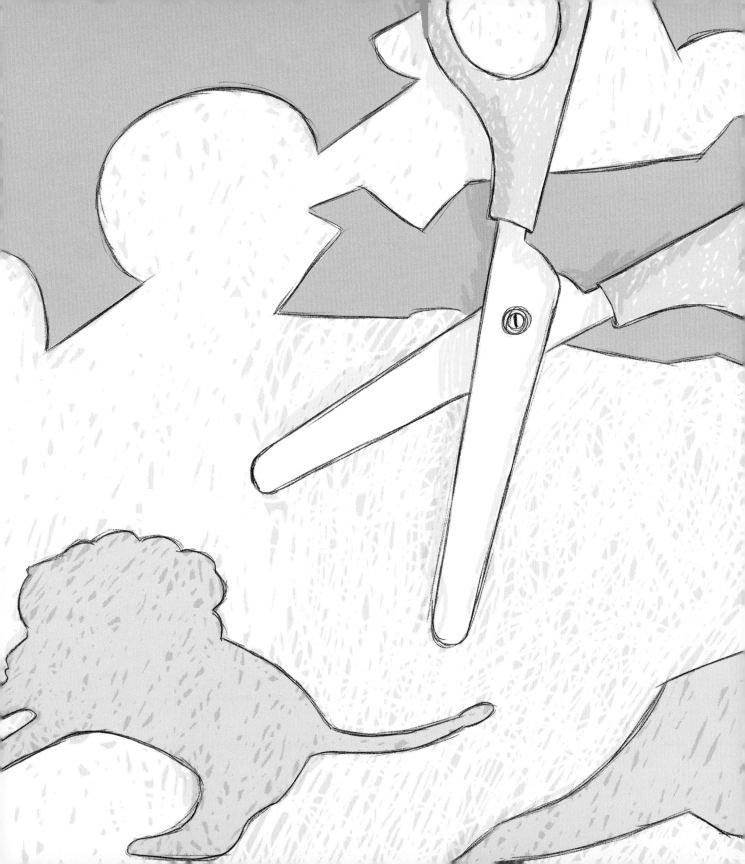

The boy sitting at the desk near the window doesn't speak.

Well, he talks at home. But not at school.

Not even a word.

"He's very shy," says his mom.

"There's something wrong with him," the other parents say.

Our teacher says
that eventually
he'll open up.

That seems like a
nice idea—as if
he were a flower.

But he isn't a flower.
He's a boy.

The days go by,
and nothing changes.

How does he stay so silent?
He spends most of the time looking out the window.
If you try to talk to him, he'll just look at you for a moment.
If you ask a question, he shrugs.

Or he nods yes or shakes his head no. That's his only answer.

the silence game

At recess I try to imagine what it feels like.
I try to act just like him, and I don't say anything for the whole morning.

The time goes slowly, so slowly.

Recess ends and I feel alone, and then the words come bursting out all at once.

I find my friend.

I talk to her, tell her a story. We sing and clap our hands, and we laugh.

What a relief.

Talking is like breathing.

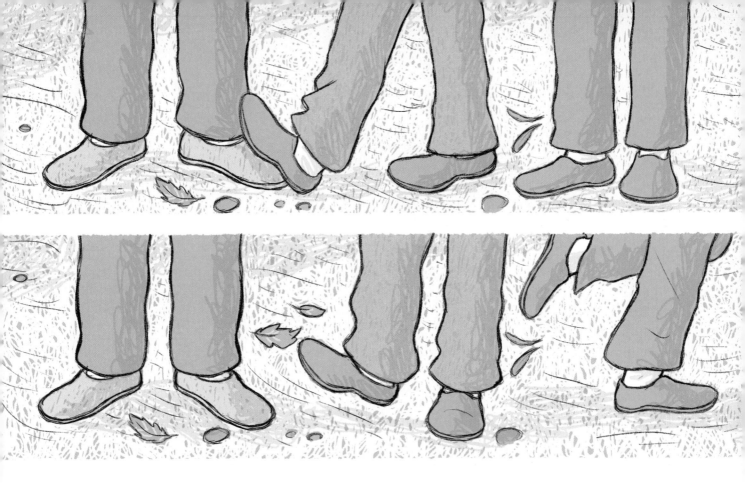

One time an older boy stepped on his foot to see what would happen.
But he didn't say anything.

"He's like a stone,"
says my friend who
collects rocks and leaves.

Oak

fir

pebbles

apple tree

thyme

But I know
that isn't true.

When we lined up at recess, I walked next to him,
and his hand was soft and warm.

If the teacher calls him to the front of class to answer a question,
we all hold our breath.
Will he talk this time?

What will his voice sound like?

But he just takes the chalk and writes his answer on the blackboard.

the process of
photosynt

Yesterday we went to the science museum.

It was full of amazing things.

My friend and I pedaled a bicycle that turned on a light bulb.

Just before we left, I noticed an aquarium in the corner.

A handset from an old telephone
was floating in the water,
with fish swimming around it.
Next to the aquarium was
another phone.

I picked up the receiver,
raised it to my ear,
and listened.

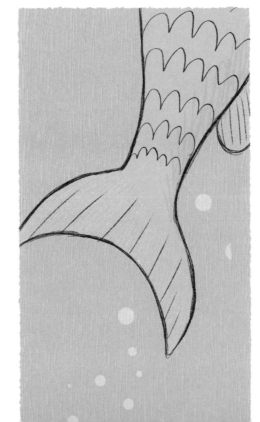

Mysterious, beautiful, secret sounds
came from the silence of the water.
My heart began to beat faster.

A sign on the wall said that fish aren't mute—they speak.
They send each other messages of danger and messages of love.

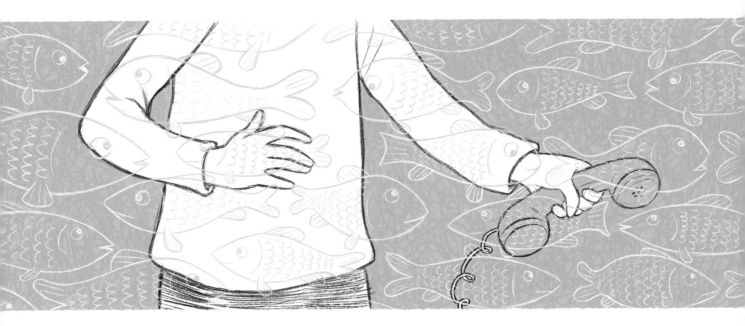

I put down the receiver and went to find my classmate.

The class was lining up, just about to leave, but he followed me anyway.
I told him what I had discovered and put the receiver to his ear.
He looked astonished.

But just then, the teacher called us.

As we headed back to school,
I thought to myself:
my friend isn't a flower.

He isn't a stone.

He is a fish
in an aquarium.

Today at school I made a drawing of a fish talking on the phone.
I folded the paper in four and passed it down the aisle
until it got to his desk.

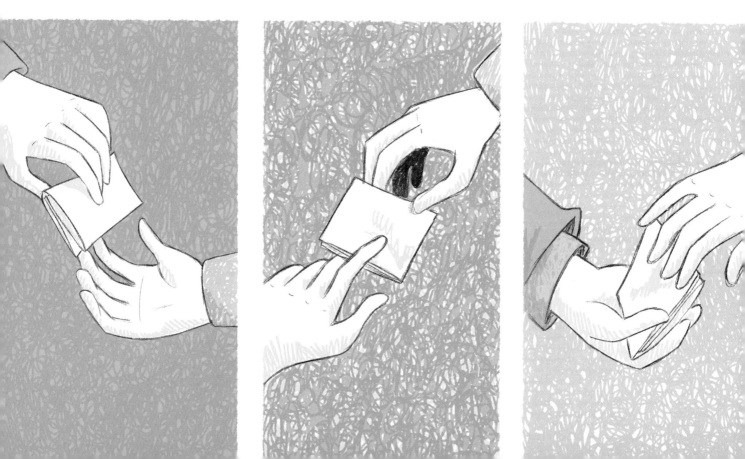

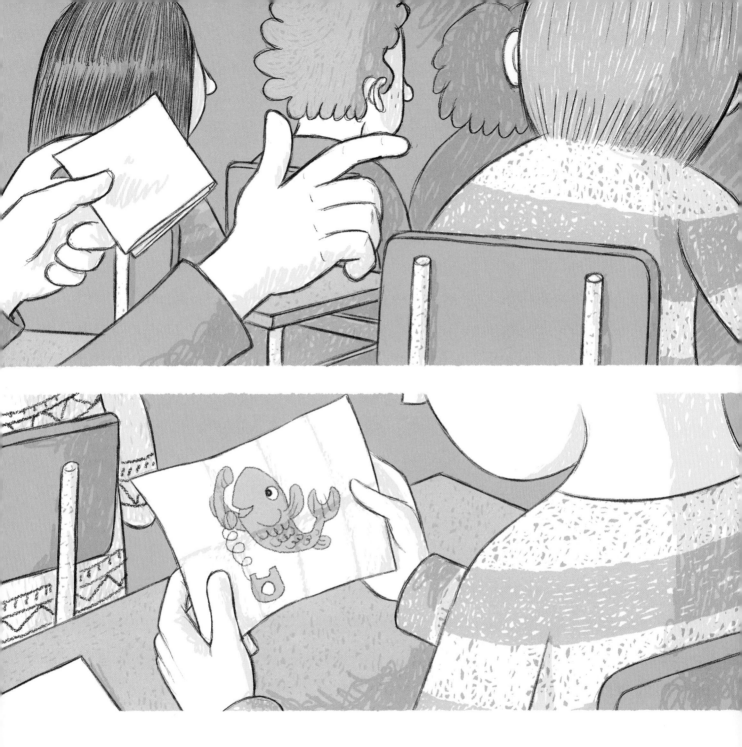

I watched him as he opened it.
Then he turned and looked at me across the classroom.

He smiled, and all my classmates faded away.

Tonight, something
extraordinary happened.

The phone rang,
and Mom said
it was for me.

I left my homework on my desk and went to answer it.
"Hello?" I said, lost in thought.

"Hi, it's me," he replied.